MUSIC MANIA

HIGHLIGHTS PRESS

Honesdale, Pennsylvania

Welcome, Hidden Pictures® Puzzlers!

When you finish a puzzle, check it off √. Good luck, and happy puzzling!

Contents

Cover Illustration by Rocky Fuller

Crocodile Rag

banana, crown, eyeglasses, fish, glove, hammer, handbell, heart, light bulb, pencil, ruler, saw, scissors, shoe, teacup, toothbrush, truck

Swing Your Partners

sailboat, baseball cap, seal, paintbrush, needle, spoon, shoe, pear, flag, open book, ice-cream cone, trowel, teacup, fishhook, hammer, radish

Illustrated by Holly Carryer

The Biggest Bagpipers

Illustrated by Arieh Zeldich

Elfin Ensemble

rabbit's head, stack of teacups, pair of shorts, sitting boy, bird's head, sock, butterfly, bird, baby in a blanket, string of sausages, dinosaur, hat, shoe, bear in a raft

Illustrated by Jeri Simkus

The Owl and the Pussycat

lantern, rowboat, elf, bat, violin, dog, dish, spoon, butterfly, frog, boot, cow

Illustrated by Malinda Schneider

Making Mountain Music

comb, snake, teacup, heart, banana, slice of apple, seashell, hammer, peanut, toothbrush, caterpillar, cotton candy, funnel

Illustrated by Ron Lieser

Practice, Practice, Practice

envelope, magnet, snow shovel, shoe, nail, ice-cream cone, banana, sailboat, flashlight, crescent moon, candle, lemon, party hat, ice-cream bar, slice of bread

Illustrated by Janet Robertson

Pet Shop Quartet

toothbrush, sneaker, glove, tweezers, light bulb, pencil, ice-cream bar, car, slice of pie, fir tree, button, heart, shoe, bell, mitten

Illustrated by Tim Davis

Illustrated by R. Michael Palan

A Mixed Chorus

mop, spoon, lollipop, candle, shoe, worm, flag, sock, vase, envelope, tack, mitten, bowl

Forest Frolic

elf's hat, mushroom, acorn, egg, cane, dolphin, pennant, seashell, feather, teacup, heart, artist's brush, four-leaf clover, chick, snake

Summertime Band

bird, sailboat, butterfly, candle, muffin, flowerpot, funnel, hammer, heart, lollipop, mitten, crescent moon, mug, needle, paintbrush, pennant, ring, shoe, spoon, toothbrush, tulip

Illustrated by Linda Weller

Night Owls

arrow, clothes hanger, comb, domino, fishhook, golf club, ice-cream cone, light bulb, vase, ring, tack, trowel

Illustrated by Arieh Zeldich

Animal Arabesque

artist's brush, pennant, hammer, leaf, magnet, mug, slice of pie, sailboat, sock, telescope, cane, funnel, heart, lollipop, crescent moon, needle, ring, snake, spoon, toothbrush

Illustrated by Rocky Fuller

Squeeze-Box Serenade

fork, slice of pie, strawberry, snail, toothbrush, needle, artist's brush, comb, fishhook, hockey stick, teacup, slice of cake, ice-cream cone, sock, beet, ruler

The Rockin' Rovers

snake, toothbrush, hockey stick, tack, artist's brush, ice-cream bar, candle, teacup, comb, crescent moon, crown, boot, spoon, needle, envelope, drinking straw, lollipop

Illustrated by R. Michael Palan

Swampland Sonata

artist's brush, banana, bird, sailboat, boot, butterfly, baseball cap, paper clip, duck, heart, ice-cream cone, pair of pants, pencil, ruler, toothbrush

Carla Crane Plays a Jig

turtle, fish, fishhook, ant, paper clip, pennant, closed umbrella, roller skate, mouse, key, iron, chicken, comb, squirrel

Illustrated by Valeri Gorbachev

Maestro Meowsic's Orchestra

bell, camera, egg, cane, hamburger, nutcracker, snail, baseball, boot, carrot, envelope, fork, house, lamp, rabbit's head

Tuning Up the Tubas

hand mirror, snail's shell, teacup, mushroom, cotton swab, cane, scissors, salamander, paper clip, hat, loaf of bread, boot

Illustrated by Susan Detwiler

Chillin' with the Cool Ones

ax, banana, can, crescent moon, feather, flying disk, ice-cream bar, key, paintbrush, present, ring, sailboat, slice of pie, teacup

Ms. Franny and the Froggies

arrow, bird, boxing glove, coat hanger, handbell, iron, key, mouse, needle and thread, pencil, roller skate, sailboat, shovel, spoon

Illustrated by Valeri Gorbachev

Illustrated by Rex Schneider

The Basset Hound Blues

star, glove, nail, fish, cane, banana, tack, mushroom, artist's brush, candle, toothbrush, crescent moon, jump rope, lollipop

Illustrated by George Wildman

Oh My Darlin' Clementine

arrow, bird, 2 hairbrushes, fish, fork, frog, glove, fishhook, mouse, paper clip, penguin, telephone receiver, turtle

Illustrated by Valeri Gorbachev

Picnic Parade

glove, egg, teapot, sneaker, fish, crown, duck, paper clip, heart, banana, hammer, straight pin, sailboat, eyeglasses

Illustrated by Tim Davis

The Fairies' River Waltz

caterpillar, comb, elf's hat, glove, light bulb, shark, mouse, banana, pencil, ring, high-heeled shoe, nail

Illustrated by Kit Wray

The Jungle Shuffle

sailboat, bell, dolphin, crescent moon, fir tree, banana, starfish, pennant, elf's hat, dog's dish, ring, candle, fishhook, domino, belt

Ode to a Toad

banana, comb, glove, slice of pie, screwdriver, snake, tea bag, wristwatch, candle, feather, hat, leaf, pliers, shell, spoon, toothbrush

Three Piggy Opera

Illustrated by Gary Mohrman

33

Hay-Bale Hootenanny

spoon, bell, hairbrush, candle, golf club, heart, ladle, mitten, musical note, paper clip, pencil, slice of cake, tube of toothpaste

Ring Around the Rosie

pencil, parrot, scarf, mouse, vase, snail, mitten, rabbit, frog, duck, fish, ruler, spoon, penguin

Illustrated by Valeri Gorbachev

A Tuba Plays in Aruba

heart, crown, bell, banana, paper clip, ice-cream cone, handbell, eyeglasses, fish, horn, pencil, egg, toothbrush, sneaker

Illustrated by Tim Davis

Music in the Meadow

sock, dinosaur, pear, radish, chili pepper, shark, needle, carrot, peapod, slice of pie, ice-cream cone, crescent moon, pencil, toothbrush, slice of pizza, mitten, slice of orange, spoon, feather

Illustrated by Janet Robertson

Minuet in G

parrot, ice-cream cone, teacup, cupcake, dog, fork, horn, penguin, rooster, seal, shoe, bird, spoon, toothbrush

Rooster's Solo

artist's brush, pencil, paper clip, dog, sailboat, banana, ice-cream cone, golf club, megaphone, nail, heart, fir tree, glove, comb, eyeglasses, spaceship, ice pop

Illustrated by Tim Davis

Air for Accordions

clothespin, pickle, arrow, shoe, needle, fish, caterpillar, mug, slice of pie, eyeglasses, Eiffel Tower, bell

Illustrated by Mary Sullivan

Alley a Cappella

Illustrated by Kathy Swain-O'Brien

The Coolest Cats in School

golf club, mallet, pencil, tack, ribbon, candle, teardrop, net, boomerang, adhesive bandage, apple, feather

Illustrated by Rocky Fuller

The Hayride Boogie

pencil, slice of pizza, bowling pin, feather, bird, teacup, mushroom, elf's hat, crescent moon, briefcase, chicken, mallet

Tweet, Tweet Music

Illustrated by David Helton

Petey and the Pets

nail, paintbrush, baby's bottle, canoe, coat hanger, spoon, ring, snake, drinking straw, fishhook, needle, golf club

Illustrated by R. Michael Palan

46

Lady Z. Sings the Blues

handbell, 2 butterflies, screw, eyeglasses, sea horse, snake, flag, candle, tack, golf ball, spatula, mug, ring, belt, seashell

Illustrated by Arieh Zeldich

Piggy Pirouettes

boot, butterfly, fish, needle, sailboat, teacup, banana, bowl, button, heart, nail, pear, snail, tube of toothpaste

The Cow Jumped

flashlight, carrot, dog bone, fried egg, open book, sock, car, bee, fish, heart, pennant, handbell, slice of bread, ice-cream cone, banana, glove, snail

Illustrated by Maggie Swanson

Woodland Fugue

sailboat, rabbit, airplane, canoe, baseball bat, key, bird, muffin, horse's head, coffeepot, king's head, headphones, cat, loaf of bread

Final Rehearsal

Illustrated by Chuck Dillon

Animals on Parade

feather, crescent moon, toothbrush, banana, paper clip, spatula, ladle, snake, bell, button, slice of pie, marshmallow, cinnamon bun

The Scottish Piper

nail, candle, bird, needle, book, ladle, golf club, slice of pie, baseball bat, tube of toothpaste, drum, crescent moon, artist's brush

Rockabilly Rabbits

banana, bee, bird, comb, dolphin, envelope, hammer, lollipop, mouse, ruler, shoe, spoon

Illustrated by Kit Wray

At the Ballet

snake, duck, crescent moon, carrot, artist's brush, shoe, tack, ice-cream cone, musical note, fishhook, spoon, candle, pencil, closed umbrella, banana

Swingin' with the Stylarks

illustrated by Ron Lieser

Furry Fanfare

ant, arrow, sailboat, chicken, clothespin, comb, mug, 2 ducks, duckling, fish, flashlight,
fork, hammer, coat hanger, ice-cream cone, iron, key, scissors, shoe, shovel, roller skate,

spoon, turtle, wrench

Illustrated by Valeri Gorbachev

Saturday at the Music Store

butterfly, slice of cake, paper clip, ice-cream bar, closed umbrella, funnel, knitted hat, fish, clothespin, toothbrush, sock, ring

Water-Bottle Band

pear, ice-cream bar, turtle, mitten, flag, candle, slipper, spoon, fish, balloon, nail, carrot, mushroom, trowel

Illustrated by Janet Robertson

62

How to Play the Accordion

test tube, olive, fork, crayon, light bulb, tweezers, slice of bread, heart, fishhook, tube of toothpaste, snail, jump rope, egg

Illustrated by Paul Richer

Bug Band

banana, baseball bat, thimble, bird, sailboat, candle, teacup, pennant, crescent moon,
ice-cream bar, ring, sock

At the Pianoforte

bolt, closed umbrella, nail, spoon, book, radish, goblet, hamburger, golf club, canoe, ax, balloon, snake, eyeglasses, otter, slice of pie, hoe, needle, saltshaker, bear, slice of cake, crayon, caterpillar, ruler

Illustrated by Elizabeth Allyn

Night at the Opera

fish, apron, rabbit's head, closed umbrella, flowerpot, teacup, apple, mouse, pail, safety pin, wrench, banana, carrot, tree, sailboat, snail, ice-cream cone, spoon

Illustrated by Lynn Adams

Frog Pond Blues

key, clothespin, needle, sheep's head, salamander, bird, bell, fish, seal, bottle, safety pin, beetle, cat's head, caterpillar

Illustrated by Mij Colson-Barnum

The Songbirds

Band in the Barn

kite, starfish, slice of pizza, spool of thread, candy corn, heart, paintbrush, spoon, ring, sock, candle, CD, book, tulip, fish, pencil

Illustrated by Susan Dahlman

Spring Recital

pennant, toothbrush, cupcake, plate, banana, crown, olive, heart, sock, tube of toothpaste, ruler, dog bone

Rockin' the Recorders

Illustrated by Paul Richer

The Pixie Drummer

ball, carrot, eyeglasses, handbell, coat hanger, ice-cream cone, nail, needle, pencil, ruler, spoon, teacup, necktie

Night Owl School

baseball bat, boomerang, candle, canoe, heart, key, mitten, needle, olive, snail, spaceship, tack, bell

Music by Moonlight

seal, mouse, bow tie, scissors, fork, stork, spoon, dragonfly, briefcase, comb, duck, sailboat, bug, pennant

Illustrated by Valeri Gorbachev

Dress Rehearsal

Toot, Toot, Toot!

sailboat, flashlight, crayon, ruler, spoon, teacup, carrot, fishhook, telescope, cowboy boot, lollipop, oven mitt, candle, cowboy hat

Illustrated by Linda Weller

Swinging under the Big Top

2 ducks, pennant, spoon, umbrella, fishhook, open book, paper clip, ice-cream cone, coat hanger, bird, candle, pear, whale

Illustrated by Valeri Gorbachev

Freddie's Fan Club

ruler, fishhook, ice pop, wishbone, banana, mug, umbrella, flag, ladle, toothbrush, tack, needle, baseball bat, mitten

Illustrated by Karen Stormer Brooks

A Rare Sighting

eyeglasses, scissors, bow tie, hairbrush, canoe, comb, crayon, fish, glove, hot dog, pliers, slice of pie

Lights, Camera, Action!

banana, bowling pin, crown, fish, key, scissors, teacup, tube of toothpaste, dog bone, comb, envelope, heart, ruler, snake, toothbrush

Illustrated by Maxim Mitrofanov

Leading the Parade

bell, crescent moon, heart, open book, tack, tube of toothpaste, artist's brush, butterfly, crown, rolling pin, teacup, worm

Illustrated by Diana Zourelias

Everybody Polka!

pencil, teacup, wedge of cheese, closed umbrella, adhesive bandage, party hat, screw, flashlight, ruler, comb, pear, candle, funnel, book, sailboat, needle, spool of thread, scissors,

ring, slice of pie, crescent moon, hammer, golf club, worm, Easter egg, magnet, pennant, mushroom, butterfly, hand mirror

Rhythm and Nursery Rhyme

fedora, beret, top hat, chef's hat, fez, sombrero, party hat, Russian fur hat, princess's hat, police officer's hat, straw hat, Robin Hood's hat, graduation cap, baseball cap, woman's hat, derby, pointy hat

Illustrated by Joe Seldita

Where Elephants Dance

fishing pole, dog, seal, peanut, gingerbread cookie, shovel, fish, ring, lamb's head, mouse, sailboat, snowman, sock, banana, doe's head, top hat, carrot

Illustrated by Jeri Simkus

Outdoor Concert

artist's brush, crown, ice-cream cone, magnifying glass, ring, spatula, book, button, pennant, kite, pencil, sailboat, tack

Gracie Goat's First Recital

Illustrated by Valeri Gorbachev

Dancers at the Barre

tube of toothpaste, slice of pie, tack, flashlight, drinking straw, mushroom, clothespin, ring, crown, toothbrush, flag, pencil

Dance Tunes

Goose and Gander Do-Si-Do

artist's brush, bird, comb, crown, nail, fish, fishhook, heart, ice-cream cone, paper clip, pencil, rabbit, sailboat, high-heeled shoe

Illustrated by Tim Davis

Practice Makes Purr-fect

apple, candle, feather, flashlight, slice of pie, flag, needle, nail, boomerang, pencil, ice-cream cone, mitten, coat hanger, belt, vase

Illustrated by Larry Daste

Barnyard Dance

oar, pushpin, 2 dominoes, shovel, hockey stick, teacup, pear, ice-cream cone, 2 hearts, hand mirror, sailboat, banana, crescent moon, boomerang, comb, coat hanger, button, cane,

cowboy boot, light bulb, bell, envelope, hammer, key, drinking glass, pitcher, ring, oyster shell, pineapple, pumpkin, golf club

McBowzer's Bagpipe Band

bell, bowl, candle, comb, crayon, eyeglasses, flashlight, coat hanger, hot dog, mug, mushroom, paintbrush, palm tree, plate, slice of bread, spool of thread

Musical Chairs

fishhook, needle, stork, lollipop, heart, bell, artist's brush, pennant, open book, crescent moon, snake, light bulb, golf club, eyeglasses, cherry

Illustrated by Arieh Zeldich

Dog the Drum Major

sock, spoon, bird, mitten, hairbrush, broom, purse, light bulb, sailboat, open book, baseball, carrot, fish, duck, squirrel, boot

Illustrated by Leslie Franz

Ollie on Alto Sax

key, fork, paper clip, arrow, comb, duck, spoon, dragonfly, mouse, snail, fishhook, coat hanger, tack, bird

Illustrated by Valeri Gorbachev

Mega Challenge! Find 15 Hidden Objects!

Illustrated by Joyce Haynes

Dancing Cheek to Cheek

banana, comb, mushroom, pennant, sailboat, snake, tube of toothpaste, bell, fishhook, nail, slice of pizza, scrub brush, tack, closed umbrella

Illustrated by Maxim Mitrofanov

Promenade, All!

artist's brush, banana, bell, book, light bulb, slice of cake, candle, paper clip, crayon, mitten, golf club, hammer, hoe, ladle, mallet, nail, needle, pen, slice of pie, pushpin, radish,

Illustrated by Charles Jordan

Cherry Blossom Song

mushroom, hockey stick, banana, slice of bread, spoon, slice of pie, shuttlecock, worm, toothbrush, star, Easter egg, spool of thread, sailboat, tack, jug, needle

Musical Mice

Illustrated by Diana Zourelias

105

The Jungle Band

key, slice of pizza, boot, mug, pencil, comb, golf club, candle, banana, heart, snake, ring, ruler, toothbrush, tack

Grizzly Trio

fork, hairbrush, key, nail, needle, penguin, ring, sailboat, shoe, shovel, slipper, spool of thread, spoon, toothbrush

Illustrated by Valeri Gorbachev

Raising the Rafters

ice-cream cone, handbell, glove, coat hanger, shoe, carrot, crown, needle, banana, pencil, toothbrush, sailboat

Dancing at the Fair

crescent moon, needle, chick, hatchet, fish, fishhook, book, toaster, slipper, dog's head, horseshoe, vase

Jam Session

needle, frying pan, flashlight, shoe, ice-cream bar, rabbit, artist's brush, woman's head, boot, pencil, crown, golf club, ice-cream cone, bird, whistle, mallet, comb

Illustrated by R. Michael Palan

Minstrels' Music

bird, open book, swan, carrot, banana, bell, pear, horse, dragonfly, envelope, butterfly, crown, cake, fork, dog

Illustrated by John Kinnaird

Ain't Misbehavin'

pencil, wristwatch, hammer, comb, coat hanger, candle, cane, golf club, wishbone, closed umbrella, artist's brush, needle, pennant, nail, toothbrush

Illustrated by R. Michael Palan

The Pied Piper

toothbrush, book, iron, pencil, banana, sailboat, paper clip, shoe, spoon, eyeglasses, handbell, nail, ruler, fish

Illustrated by Tim Davis

Stompin' in the Swamp

artist's brush, crescent moon, egg, needle, pearl necklace, tepee, apple, bottle, doughnut, golf club, nail, peanut, spoon, closed umbrella

Illustrated by Rocky Fuller

A Little Mice Music

fork, bird, sock, nail, lollipop, toothbrush, heart, hammer, snake, fishhook, crown, tennis ball, trowel, strawberry

The Strummers

feather, ring, candle, pencil, crown, mushroom, dog bone, slice of pizza, snake, wristwatch, bowl, egg, bell, teacup, apple, nail, seal

Illustrated by Diana Zourelias

A Welcome Song

otter, fish, dolphin, lion, envelope, ant, snake, 2 birds, boot, cane, hammer, man's head

Illustrated by Kit Wray

Aria for Little Bird

Illustrated by Susan Dahlman

Recital Jitters

teacup, spoon, dog bone, comb, saltshaker, pencil, slice of pizza, snail, paper clip, flashlight, wishbone, fish, crescent moon

Illustrated by Maggie Swanson

Miss Milly's Dance Studio

pencil, golf club, pennant, sailboat, spoon, heart, pear, mushroom, hockey stick, tack, snake, light bulb, butterfly, cherry, strawberry

Illustrated by Arieh Zeldich

Dancing at the Hoedown

banana, coffeepot, funnel, caterpillar, hatchet, kite, mitten, crescent moon, ruler, screwdriver, shoe, butter knife

Two to Tango

snail, bowl, horseshoe, padlock, musical note, slice of pizza, moth, needle, leaf, lightning bolt, horn, crescent moon, mushroom, heart, whale

Illustrated by Diana Zourelias

Dixieland Band

rabbit, boomerang, golf club, straight pin, coat hanger, balloon, hockey stick, cane, fishhook, ring, waffle, comb, ax, key, domino, yo-yo, lollipop

Illustrated by Arieh Zeldich

All Together Now

cane, pennant, funnel, hammer, heart, leaf, lollipop, magnet, crescent moon, mug, needle, artist's brush, slice of pie, ring, sailboat, snake, sock, spoon, telescope, toothbrush

Illustrated by Rocky Fuller

Bob and the Bow-Wows

pear, ice pop, mug, carrot, coat hanger, pencil, broom, tack, ring, book, golf club, key, fish

126

Illustrated by R. Michael Palan

Learning the Kangaroo Hop

mallet, football, screw, tube of toothpaste, handbell, crescent moon, kite, boomerang, crown, shovel, butterfly, mug, hot-air balloon

Illustrated by Arieh Zeldich

The Beaver Bounce

Illustrated by Valeri Gorbachev

Wynton Bearsalis

turtle, sheep, fish, broom, lighthouse, wishbone, toy top, toothbrush, cowboy boot, teddy bear, hat, flashlight, telescope, rolling pin

Illustrated by Carol Sutherby

Circus Parade

balloon, open book, spoon, mop, teacup, life preserver, handbell, hammer, hat, tack, table, hairbrush, ring, toothbrush, boot, crescent moon

Illustrated by R. Michael Palan

▼Page 4

▼Page 5

▼Page 6

▼Page 7

▼Page 8

▼Page 9

▼Page 10

▼Page 11

▼Page 12

Answers

▼Page 13

▼Page 14

▼Page 15

▼Page 16

▼Page 17

▼Page 18

▼Page 19

▼Page 20

▼Page 21

132

Answers

▼Page 22

▼Page 23

▼Page 24

▼Page 25

▼Page 26

▼Page 27

▼Page 28

▼Page 29

▼Page 30

Answers

▼Page 31

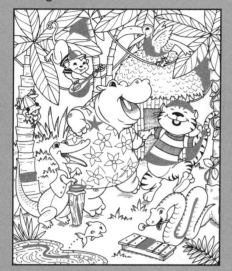

▼Page 32

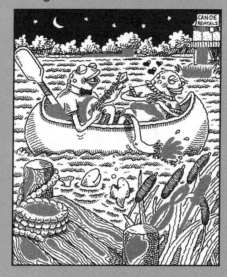

▼Page 33

▼Page 34

▼Page 35

▼Page 36

▼Page 37

▼Page 38

▼Page 39

Answers

▼Page 40

▼Page 41

▼Pages 42–43

▼Page 44

▼Page 45

▼Page 46

▼Page 47

Answers

▼Page 48

▼Page 49

▼Page 50

▼Page 51

▼Pages 52–53

▼Page 54

▼Page 55

▼Page 56

▼ Page 57

▼ Pages 58–59

▼ Pages 60–61

▼ Page 62

▼ Page 63

▼ Page 64

▼ Page 65

Answers

▼ Page 66

▼ Page 67

▼ Page 68

▼ Page 69

▼ Pages 70–71

▼ Page 72

▼ Page 73

▼ Page 74

▼Page 75

▼Pages 76–77

▼Page 78

▼Page 79

▼Page 80

▼Page 81

▼Page 82

▼Page 83

Answers

▼ Pages 84–85

▼ Page 86

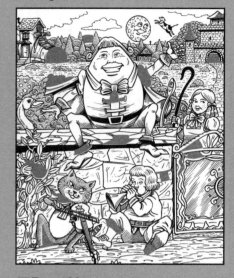

▼ Page 87

▼ Page 88

▼ Page 89

▼ Pages 90–91

▼ Page 92

Answers

▼Page 93

▼Pages 94–95

▼Page 96

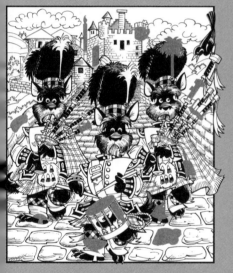

▼Page 97

▼Page 98

▼Page 99

▼Page 100

▼Page 101

Answers

▼Pages 102–103

▼Page 104

▼Page 105

▼Page 106

▼Page 107

▼Pages 108–109

▼Page 110

Answers

▼Page 111

▼Page 112

▼Page 113

▼Page 114

▼Page 115

▼Page 116

▼Page 117

▼Page 118

▼Page 119

Answers

▼Page 120

▼Page 121

▼Page 122

▼Page 123

▼Page 124

▼Page 125

▼Page 126

▼Page 127

▼Page 128